ZENDAYA

ACTING ★ SUPERSTAR

REBECCA FELIX

Big Buddy Books

An Imprint of Abdo Publishing
abdobooks.com

ABDOBOOKS.COM

Published by Abdo Publishing, a division of ABDO, PO Box 398166, Minneapolis, Minnesota 55439.
Copyright © 2022 by Abdo Consulting Group, Inc. International copyrights reserved in all countries.
No part of this book may be reproduced in any form without written permission from the publisher.
Big Buddy Books™ is a trademark and logo of Abdo Publishing.

Printed in the United States of America, North Mankato, Minnesota

052021
092021

 THIS BOOK CONTAINS RECYCLED MATERIALS

Design: Kelly Doudna, Mighty Media, Inc.
Production: Mighty Media, Inc.
Editor: Liz Salzmann
Cover Photograph: Shutterstock Images
Interior Photographs: Abaca Press/AP Images, pp. 23, 29 (bottom); Alison Yin/AP Images, p. 9; Craig Sjodin/Getty Images, p. 15; Earl Gibson III/Getty Images, p. 7; Matt Sayles/AP Images, p. 17; Shutterstock Images, pp. 5, 11, 13, 19, 21, 25, 27, 29 (top, center); Sthanlee B. Mirador/AP Images, pp. 1, 28

Library of Congress Control Number: 2020949914

Publisher's Cataloging-in-Publication Data

Names: Felix, Rebecca, author.
Title: Zendaya: acting superstar / by Rebecca Felix
Other title: acting superstar
Description: Minneapolis, Minnesota : Abdo Publishing, 2022 | Series: Superstars | Includes online resources and index.
Identifiers: ISBN 9781532195693 (lib. bdg.) | ISBN 9781098216429 (ebook)
Subjects: LCSH: Zendaya (Zendaya Coleman), 1996- --Juvenile literature. | Actresses--United States--Biography--Juvenile literature. | Television actors and actresses--United States--Biography--Juvenile literature. | Motion picture actors and actresses--United States--Biography--Juvenile literature. | Women--Biography--Juvenile literature.
Classification: DDC 791.450--dc23

CONTENTS

ZENDAYA

Zendaya is a dancer, singer, actor, and model. She has worked on famous fashion projects.

Zendaya has earned many honors for her talents. And across her work, she encourages **diversity**.

—Zendaya on using only her first name as her stage name

Zendaya's name is pronounced Zen-DAY-uh.

FAMILY & SCHOOL

Zendaya Maree Stoermer Coleman was born on September 1, 1996. She grew up in Oakland, California. Her mother, Claire Stoermer, and her father, Kazembe Ajamu Coleman, were teachers.

Kazembe has five children from an earlier marriage. These are Zendaya's half-brothers and half-sisters.

Zendaya (*center*) with her parents in 2016

At home, Zendaya liked to sing and dance. But at school, she was very shy. Zendaya rarely spoke in kindergarten. This held her back. So, she repeated kindergarten. This gave her a chance to practice her social skills.

Kazembe helped Zendaya get over her shyness. When Zendaya was eight, she sang with him in a school concert. Once Zendaya got onstage, she liked it! It was the first of many performances in her life.

Zendaya went on a concert tour in 2012. It was called the Swag It Out tour.

YOUNG ENTERTAINER

Zendaya continued performing. She joined **hip-hop** dance group Future Shock Oakland. Zendaya also performed at the California Shakespeare Theater.

Then, Zendaya started working as a model. In 2009, she appeared in a TV ad for Sears stores.

In 2019, Zendaya modeled in ads for a perfume called Idôle.

In 2010, Zendaya got a part in the Disney Channel TV show *Shake It Up*. Her character's name was Rocky Blue.

Some of the songs Zendaya sang on *Shake It Up* became popular. One of them was "Watch Me." She sang this song with costar Bella Thorne. The song reached number 86 on the *Billboard* Hot 100 music chart!

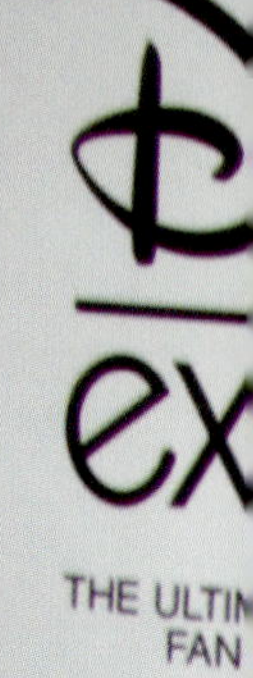

Zendaya (*left*) and Bella Thorne attended an event for Disney fans in 2011.

SONG & DANCE

While continuing her acting work, Zendaya also recorded music. She released the album *Zendaya* in 2013. The same year, Zendaya appeared on the dance contest show *Dancing with the Stars*. She and her dancing partner finished in second place.

SUPERSTAR ★ SCOOP

Zendaya was 16 when she was on *Dancing with the Stars*. At the time, she was the youngest person to be on the show!

Zendaya's partner on *Dancing with the Stars* was professional dancer Valentin Chmerkovskiy.

YOUNG PRODUCER

In 2015, Zendaya appeared in another Disney Channel show, *K.C. Undercover*. Zendaya required that the show feature a family of color. She wanted to increase **diversity** on TV. Zendaya was also named as a **producer** of the show!

Zendaya (*right*) won a Kids' Choice Award for favorite female TV star in a kids' show for her role in *K.C. Undercover*.

ACTIVISM

At the 2015 Academy Awards, Zendaya wore her hair in **dreadlocks**. A reporter made negative comments about the hairstyle. Zendaya responded that the comments were **racist**.

Fans and fellow entertainers praised her for speaking out. Soon after, toy company Mattel released a Barbie doll with dreadlocks that looked like Zendaya! This was to honor her **activism**.

Zendaya holds her Barbie doll at a Barbie-themed concert sponsored by Mattel.

FASHION & FILMS

In 2016, Zendaya became a CoverGirl model. She also released the song "Something New" that year and started a fashion line called Daya.

Meanwhile, Zendaya starred in her first major movie. She played MJ in the 2017 film *Spider-Man: Homecoming*.

SUPERSTAR ★ SCOOP

Zendaya had certain goals for her fashion line, Daya. She wanted its items to be affordable and made in many sizes.

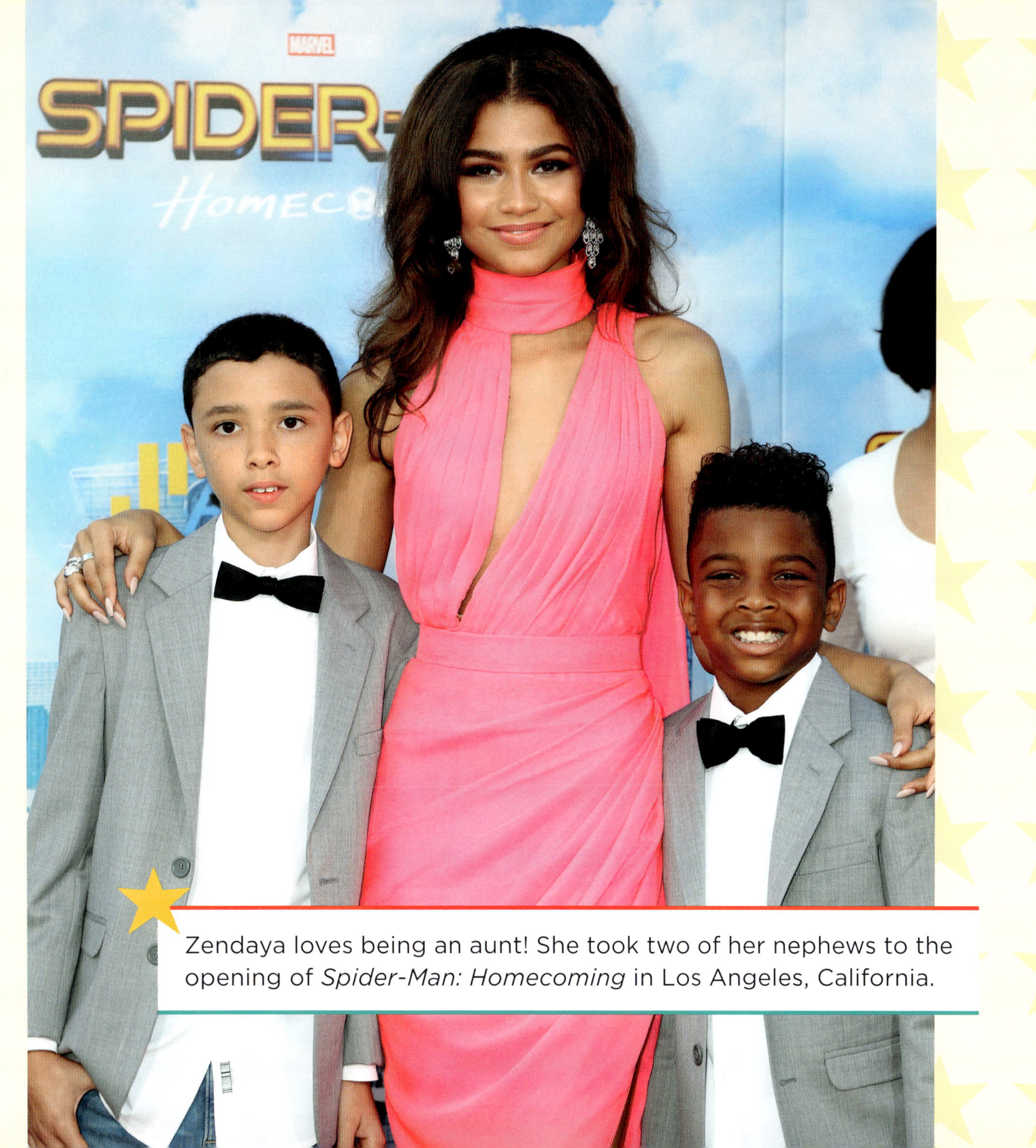

Zendaya loves being an aunt! She took two of her nephews to the opening of *Spider-Man: Homecoming* in Los Angeles, California.

Also in 2017, Zendaya played a **trapeze** artist in *The Greatest Showman*. She practiced on the trapeze and performed many of her own stunts. She also sang "Rewrite the Stars" with costar Zac Efron.

In 2018, Zendaya voiced characters in two **animated** movies, *Smallfoot* and *Duck Duck Goose*. The next year, she played MJ again in *Spider-Man: Far from Home*.

Zendaya and Efron both won Teen Choice Awards for their performances in *The Greatest Showman*.

MAKING HISTORY

In 2019, Zendaya returned to TV in the show *Euphoria*. It had a more serious story than her other projects. She played Rue, a recovering drug **addict**.

Zendaya's performance earned her an Emmy Award! She won Outstanding Lead Actress in a Drama Series. She was the youngest person and second Black actor to win this award.

Zendaya (*third from left*) with fellow members of the *Euphoria* cast

POSITIVE PLATFORM

Zendaya is passionate about social justice. She often talks about the need for positive change. She encourages her fans to speak up too. Zendaya is famous for performing. But she says she also wants to be known as a good person.

SUPERSTAR ★ SCOOP

In 2018, Zendaya started working with fashion **designer** Tommy Hilfiger on the Tommy x Zendaya collection.

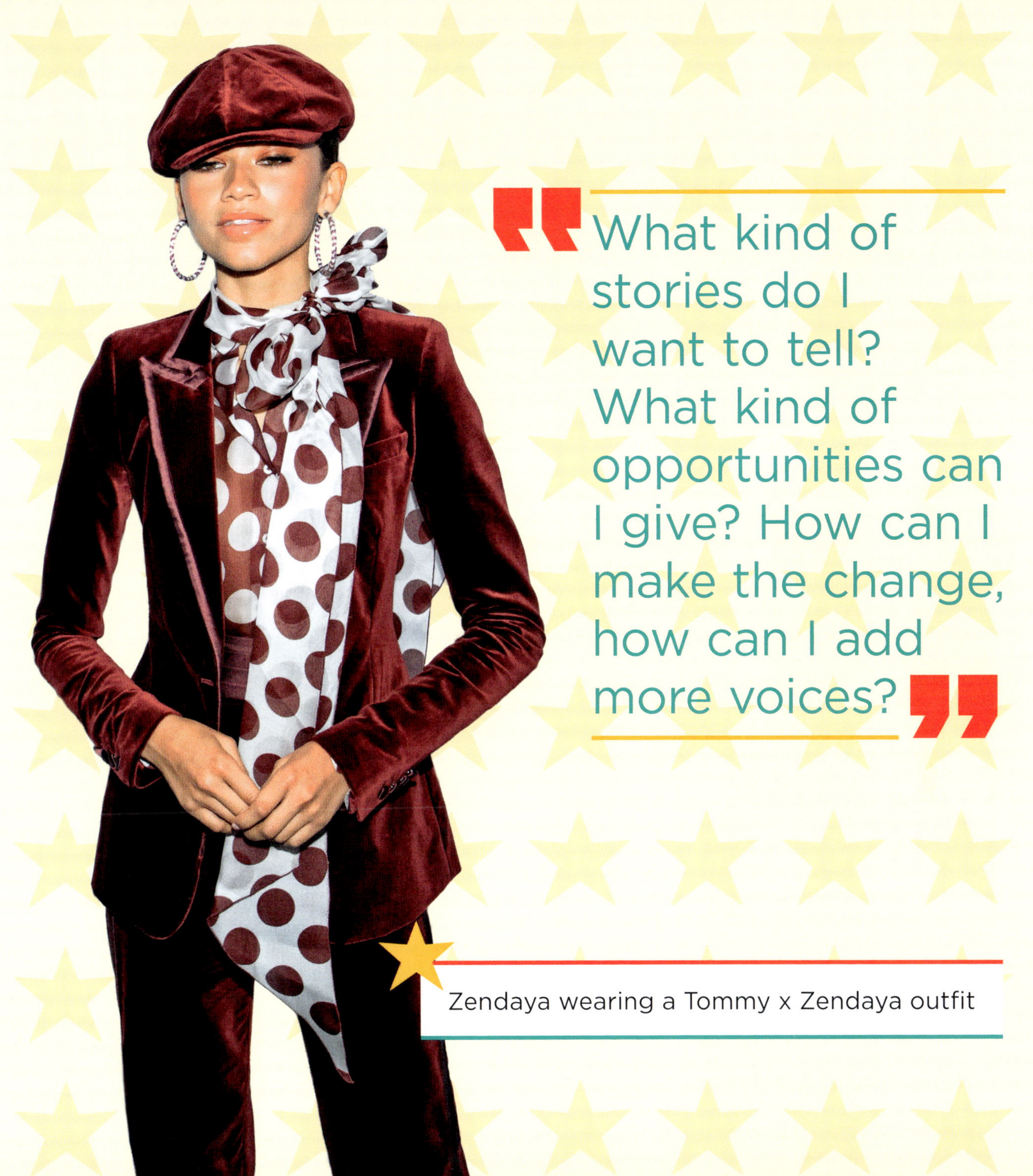

Zendaya wearing a Tommy x Zendaya outfit

TIMELINE

Zendaya Maree Stoermer Coleman was born on September 1 in Oakland, California.

1996

2009

Zendaya appeared in a Sears TV commercial.

Zendaya got a part in the Disney Channel TV show *Shake It Up*.

2010

2015

Zendaya appeared in Disney Channel's TV show *K.C. Undercover*. She was also a producer of the show.

Zendaya appeared in the movies *Spider-Man: Homecoming* and *The Greatest Showman*.

2017

Zendaya became the youngest person to win the Emmy Award for Lead Actress in a Drama for her role in *Euphoria*.

2020

2018

Zendaya voiced characters in the movies *Smallfoot* and *Duck Duck Goose*.

2019

Zendaya appeared in *Spider-Man: Far from Home* and in the TV show *Euphoria*.

GLOSSARY

activism—working for or speaking up about a cause or issue you believe in.

addict—someone who has a strong need or want for a substance, activity, or other thing.

animated—made using drawings instead of live actors.

designer (dih-ZYNE-ur)—someone who plans how something will appear or work.

diversity—having people of different races or cultures.

dreadlocks—a hairstyle made using narrow ropelike strands of hair formed by braiding or twisting.

hip-hop—a form of popular music that features rhyme, spoken words, and electronic sounds. It is similar to rap music.

producer—a person who oversees the making of a movie, a play, an album, or a radio or TV show.

racist (RAY-sist)—characterized by the belief that one race is better than another.

trapeze—a high, swinging bar that acrobats perform tricks on, usually at a circus.

To learn more about Zendaya, please visit **abdobooklinks.com** or scan this QR code. These links are routinely monitored and updated to provide the most current information available.